J-ER
BYARS

Byars, Betsy Cromer.

Boo's surprise.

| DATE | | | |
|------|--|--|--|
| | | | |
| | | | |
| | | | |
| | | | |
| | | | |
| | | | |
| | | | |
| | | | |
| | | | |
| | | | |
| | | | 9/09 |

# Boo's Surprise

## Betsy Byars

### Illustrated by Erik Brooks

✦

An Early Chapter Book

Henry Holt and Company ✦ New York

*For Perry and Bright*
*—E. B.*

Henry Holt and Company, LLC
*Publishers since 1866*
175 Fifth Avenue
New York, New York 10010
www.HenryHoltKids.com

Henry Holt® is a registered trademark of Henry Holt and Company, LLC.
Text copyright © 2009 by Betsy Byars
Illustrations copyright © 2009 by Erik Brooks
Distributed in Canada by H. B. Fenn and Company Ltd.

Library of Congress Cataloging-in-Publication Data
Byars, Betsy Cromer.
Boo's surprise / Betsy Byars ; illustrated by Erik Brooks. — 1st ed.
p.    cm.
Sequel to: Boo's dinosaur.
Summary: Boo finds an egg that hatches into a new dinosaur.
ISBN 978-0-8050-8817-5
[1. Imagination—Fiction.  2. Brothers and sisters—Fiction.  3. Dinosaurs—Fiction.]
I. Brooks, Erik, ill.  II. Title.
PZ7.B9836Bos 2009   [E]—dc22     2008048849

First Edition—2009
Printed in June 2009 in the United States of America by
Worzalla, Stevens Point, Wisconsin, on acid-free paper. ∞
1  3  5  7  9  10  8  6  4  2

# Contents

# 1

# The Surprise

Boo ran into the house. "A dinosaur! A new dinosaur!" she shouted.

"Not another one," her brother, Sammy, said.

"Sammy, this was so exciting," Boo said. "I was sitting in the tree reading a book."

"That was exciting—reading a book in a tree? I do that all the time."

"I'm getting to the exciting part," said
Boo. "I was reading my book, and I heard a
very, very heavy thump behind the trees."

"Something was behind the trees?"

"Yes, and I knew it was a dinosaur
because the thump was very, very loud. I
have heard dinosaurs thump like that
before."

"So you went behind the trees and there it was. Big deal," said Sammy.

"No! Wait! I haven't gotten to the exciting part. I climbed down the tree as fast as I could. Then I ran through the trees as fast as I could," said Boo.

"And there it was," said Sammy.

"No! It was gone. Now I'm getting to the exciting part."

"Please do."

"This dinosaur left me a big surprise."

"What?"

"A giant egg!"

## 2

# The Giant Egg

"Does anybody know anything about hatching an egg?" Boo asked.

Nobody answered. Mom was cracking eggs into a bowl. Dad was reading the paper.

Boo continued, "Suppose a person had an egg . . ."

Sammy looked at her. "A *giant* egg?"

"Oh, all right, a giant egg," Boo said. "Suppose a person found a giant egg. How would she get it to hatch?"

"I don't know anything about hatching eggs. I just know how to cook them," said Mom as she cracked another egg.

Dad looked up from his paper. "I heard a noise like that in the middle of the night," he said. "It was so loud it woke me up. It came from that field behind the trees. Maybe it was a rifle shot or—"

Boo did not wait for the rest. She jumped up.

"Boo, where are you going?" asked Mom. "You haven't eaten your breakfast."

"I'll eat later," Boo called as she ran out the door.

## 3
# Dinny

"Sammy, are you busy?" Boo asked.

"Yes, I am," Sammy said. "I am reading a book. Do you want to listen?"

"I do want to listen, but I can't. I have to ask you something. It's very important."

"Go ahead. Ask."

"Well, remember one time you told me

you had a friend that no one but you could see?" asked Boo.

"I remember. His name was Peanut."

"Yes, and did Peanut want to go places with you?"

"He did go places with me. We had a great time at the beach," said Sammy.

"But did he go everywhere with you?" asked Boo.

"Not everywhere," said Sammy.

"Because Dinny—that is my new dinosaur's name—wants to go everywhere with me. He follows me. He thinks I am his mother. Did Peanut ever think you were his mother?"

"Peanut never thought I was his mother. I was his friend."

"So what did you and Peanut do?"

"Oh, sometimes we talked."

"Dinny knows only one word and that's mama."

"Sometimes we played games."

"That's it!" Boo cried. "Thank you. Thank you. Thank you."

# 4

# Dinosaur Games

"What are you doing, Boo?" Sammy cried.

"Games! Games! I have got to have games!" Boo shouted.

"Mom! Mom! Boo has thrown all my games on the floor! She has ruined all my games!"

Mom came to the door. "Boo, what are you doing?"

"Mom, I have to have games!" said Boo.
"Why?"

"My dinosaur needs games."

"I thought your dinosaur was only two days old," said Mom.

"He is, but he is already too big for hopscotch and jump rope and crack the whip."

"How about hide-and-seek?"

"He's playing that right now. Look out the window."

"Boo, you must put those games back in their boxes right now," said Mom.

"Mom, Dinny's waiting."

"Right now, Boo."

Boo turned to the window. "I'll be out as soon as I can," she called. "We'll play hopscotch again—or maybe cowboys."

Boo sat down on the floor.

"Oh, I'll help," Sammy said.

"Thank you," Boo said. "You can play cowboys with us if you like."

"I'll pass," said Sammy.

## 5

# The Lucky Camera

"Don't be mad at me, Sammy. Please, please, please, please, please!"

"Why would I be mad at you?" asked Sammy.

"Because of what I did," said Boo.

"Have you been at my games again?"

Boo shook her head.

"Then what?" asked Sammy.

"First promise you won't be mad."

"Oh, all right, I won't get mad."

"I borrowed your camera," said Boo.

"My new camera? My birthday camera?"

"I wanted to take a picture of Dinny. A lot of people don't believe I have a dinosaur. Are you mad?"

"Not yet. Is there more?"

"I had it all set up, Sammy. Dinny posed. It was perfect. He was like a statue. Then I raised the camera to my face, and I guess he thought I was going to put it in my mouth. He thought it was something to eat."

"What happened to my camera?" Sammy gasped. "Did he put my new camera in his mouth? Did he eat it?"

"He did put it in his mouth, but he didn't like the taste. He spit it out and ran away." Boo sighed. "So I didn't get the picture. I just wasn't lucky this time."

She looked at her brother. "But you were!"

"Me? How was I lucky?"

"Sammy, now you have the only camera in the world that almost took a picture of a dinosaur!" She handed him the camera. "Here."

Sammy took his camera and looked it over.

"Thank you," he said.

# 6
# The Magic Cape

Boo ran into the house. "My magic cape!
Where is my magic cape?"

"Not the magic cape again," Dad said.

"Mom, have you seen my magic cape?"

"I think it's in the washing machine with
the other towels."

"Mom! You washed my magic cape?

Maybe you washed out the magic. I won't be able to fly anymore."

"No, here it is. The magic—and the dirt—are still inside."

Boo tied the magic cape around her neck.
"Where are you going?" Sammy asked.
"To play more games with your dinosaur?"

"Yes! And this time I'm going to teach him
something useful, something I'm really
good at."

"What?" asked Sammy.

"How to fly of course," said Boo.

"Does he have a magic cape?"

"He doesn't need one, Sammy. He has wings. He just doesn't know how to use them yet. I'm going to show him."

Boo ran off. Her magic cape flew behind her.

"Then we can play flying games. We can race and play tag. I am the luckiest girl in the world."

# 7

# The Secret Whistle

"My dinosaur is gone," Boo said.

"Flew away, huh?" Sammy said.

"Yes, I knew it was going to happen. He was flying so fast. I just couldn't keep up with him."

"Are you sad, Boo?"

"Not really, because guess what?"

"I can't."

"Before he left he showed me a secret dinosaur whistle," said Boo.

"And every time you do this secret whistle, I suppose a dinosaur will come," said Sammy.

"Yes!"

"I would like to learn that myself," said Sammy.

"Okay, I'll teach you, Sammy, if—"

"If what?"

"If you lend me your camera," said Boo.

"What are you going to take a picture of? Your dinosaur is gone."

"I want to take a picture of something to remember him by."

"Like what? The grass he walked on, the air he breathed, the sky he flew in?"

Boo laughed. "Don't be silly. I want to take a picture of the eggshell he hatched out of. So can I borrow it? Please, please, please?"

"I'll take that picture for you," Sammy said.

"Thank you, thank you, thank you," Boo said. "Now I'll have two things to remember Dinny by—a picture and a secret whistle. I am—"

"I know, I know! The luckiest girl in the world!" Sammy said as they went to get the camera together.

# Other chapter books you might enjoy